This book is dedicated to everyone who helped make it possible.
Kindness and generosity are, indeed, your superpowers. Thank you.

—Marty

Text and Illustration Copyright © 2021 Marty Kelley

SLEEPING BEAR PRESS™
2395 South Huron Parkway, Suite 200
Ann Arbor, MI 48104
www.sleepingbearpress.com

Printed and bound in the United States.

10 9 8 7 6 5 4 3 2 1

Library of Congress Cataloging-in-Publication Data

Names: Kelley, Marty, author, illustrator.
Title: A cape! / written and illustrated by Marty Kelley.
Description: Ann Arbor, Michigan : Sleeping Bear Press, [2021] | Audience:
Ages 6-10. | Summary: When a boy finds a cape he knows it must mean he has a
superpower, but dad is far too distracted to play, until the boy discovers he does have a
superpower—a super powerful imagination that is far too mighty for dad to resist.
Identifiers: LCCN 2020040510 | ISBN 9781534111110 (hardcover)
Subjects: CYAC: Imagination—Fiction.
Classification: LCC PZ7.K28172 Cap 2021 | DDC [E]—dc23
LC record available at https://lccn.loc.gov/2020040510

A CAPE!

BY MARTY KELLEY

I have a cape.

If I have a cape, I must have a superpower!

Everybody knows that.

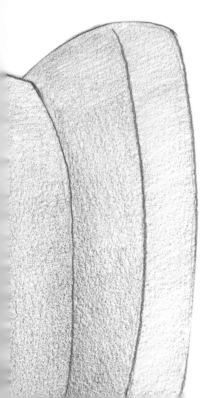

Mmmmmmhmmm.

Maybe I have super strength!
Watch me lift the couch over my head.

One...

Two...

You're going to hurt yourself.

I must be able to turn invisible!

Schwoooooosh!

You can't see me.

Yes, I can.

Please don't jump on the couch.

I can probably read minds.
Think of something and I'll tell you
what you're thinking about.

A cape?

A jet pack?

A cookie as
big as a house?

Are you using some
kind of force field
to block my powers?

No.

No.

No.

No.

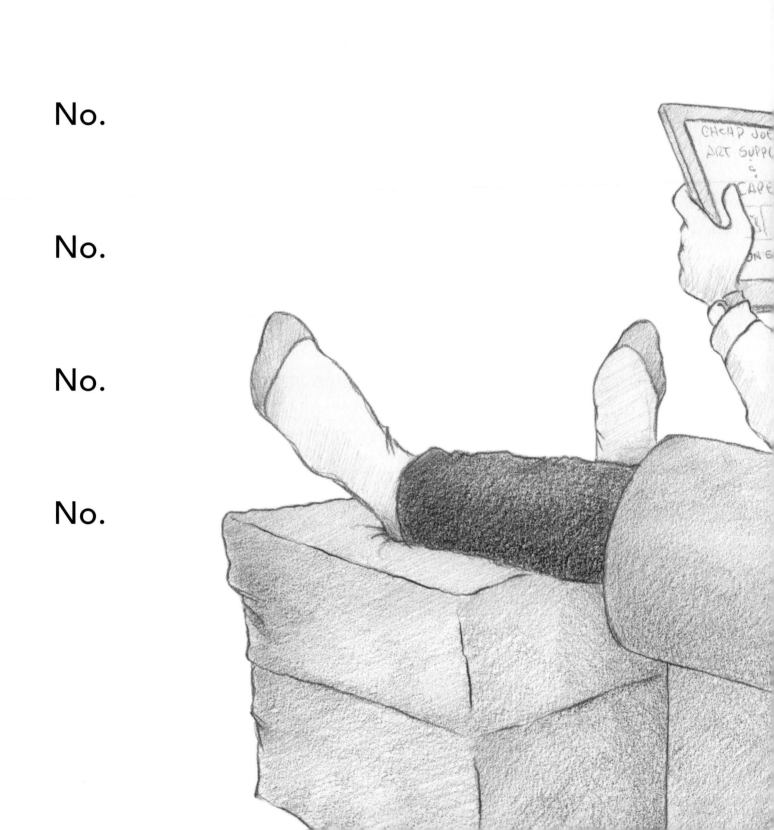

FFFFF!

Did you brush your teeth
today, young man?

Watch me run faster than a jet-powered cheetah wearing turbo-rocket sneakers!

No running in the house.

But...

I have a cape.

I must have some kind of superpower.

Well, you have a super powerful imagination.
Not everybody has that.

YEAH. That's right.
Do you know what I'm imagining now?

No. What?